The Electronic Dictator

Index:

Chapter 1: The City

This is the story of a city several centuries in the future, ruled under an iron fist. It was a dark alleyway with thick stones forming the floor, low-rise buildings on either side, and to the left of the entrance, a wooden food cart serving cheap ramen to passersby. There, a young man named Alvaro, 18 years old, sits in a red synthetic leather armchair.

—A Ramen, please, said the young Alvaro.

—It will be a moment, replied the old man as he served the food mixture in a bowl.

It was not too late, but the night was already deep. It was easy to see the small food cart with its internal lights, which illuminated more than the public lighting. On one of the large screens scattered throughout the city, the figure of the great leader Juan Costana could be seen, pronouncing phrases such as "Be careful, criminals are circulating at this hour," "Juan Costana wishes you a good day."

—Here you are — he says as he passes the plate to Alvaro.

Alvaro licks his lips as he sees it and responds with thanks, before beginning to eat peacefully. But some men approach with less peaceful intentions. They are three and do not seem very friendly to Alvaro's eyes, who realizes this after hearing the footsteps approaching the food cart and him.

—Come with us for a moment — says one of the three.

Alvaro swallows and responds:

—What do you want from me?

The man pushes him to the ground and dictates:

—You will have to come with us.

—Who are you!

After this, a fourth man, with a calmer appearance, appears behind them.

—I am Phoenix — leader of AJC.

Alvaro says nothing, he has gotten himself into a big problem, it is the only thing he is thinking about at the moment, he tries not to make the situation worse with his words, so he allows the man to speak without interrupting.

—Alvaro, you don't know me, but I do know your parents, Sofia and Lucas. They were part of the Juan Costana project, and I know what happened to them.

Alvaro's pupils widened and his lips parted, this brings back a bitter but expected memory. Seeing his parents again has been one of his biggest goals.

—Do you know about them? Tell me, please — he says expectantly.

—I personally do not know about them, but the Juan Costana AI does. Join us. As I said, we are AJC, the Anti Juan Costana organization. Our goal is to end the dictatorship of the AI and form a fair and human government.

—Down with Juancostanism! the men behind Phoenix can be heard shouting.

—Then how will I know about them if only the AI knows, and you want to destroy it?!

—Once deactivated, we will have access to the AI's database and will be able to discover what has happened to all those who have disappeared, their location, as well as other data that we have been waiting for a long time. Join us. You have no alternative, just as we have known about you, Juan Costana also knows, and it won't be long until you are arrested.

Alvaro doesn't know what to do, he is in a situation between a rock and a hard place, joining and believing that they are looking for him or trying to flee and possibly ending up worse.

—My parents were part of the project, okay, but what do I have to do with it?

—It's your voice, Alvaro, along with a song that you will surely remember, both are the key to activating something, we don't know what, but we know that if they find you it will be terrible for us and obviously for you.

Alvaro started to sweat on his forehead. Phoenix extended his hand to him.

—Okay, I'll join. He said, unsure of it.

The four men accompanied him to the main headquarters, the underground back room of a small active hair salon. There, a young 21-year-old boy, Romeo, leader of a sub-gang responsible for various tasks, was waiting.

—This is Romeo. He will be in charge of you — Phoenix said.

—Romeo, this is Lucas. Referring to Alvaro - Lucas, that will be your name from now on, it will avoid attracting attention to you, remember to use it at all times.

—It's a pleasure, by the way, you look very young, what age are you?

—I turned 18 almost a year ago.

—A real young boy — Romeo laughed.

—Romeo, be attentive to him, he is of high importance to our organization, make sure he is safe, tell Vera and Tomás clearly.

—Okay, okay — he repeated — I will treat him like one of us, he will be safe under my command.

—I hope so.

The now Lucas kept looking from one to the other as they spoke, he didn't know how to act, he was scared, and he felt uncomfortable, but he supposed it was normal, the most normal thing for sure.

They say goodbye to Phoenix and Romeo takes Lucas with him.

—The city screens can be heard in the background, but they don't say anything of interest. In a fairly low-quality shelter, Vera and Tomás are waiting.

—Are you the new one that Phoenix was talking about? — Vera asks.

—I must be.

Romeo puts his arm around Lucas's neck and in a friendly gesture, says to the other two: "It seems he is of great importance to the gang, treat him with respect.

Tomás was a little indisposed to this, he was suspicious of adding unknown people to his small group, he thought that with them it was enough. On the other hand, Vera was happy, although she felt that it was not a girl, to have a new friend.

It is late and everyone goes to bed. It is a bit cold, but Lucas manages to fall asleep despite the stress and fatigue.

—Everyone up, Romeo says. Today it's our turn to distribute Juliet.

—Juliet?

Don't make any jokes, or I'll break your arm. It's the name of the latest designer drug, it's sold like hot chestnuts.

—Okay, okay, I didn't say anything — Lucas responded.

The four boys split into two groups; Lucas and Tomás and Romeo with Lucas. Lucas saw what it was like to have the monkey for the first time in his life, he had heard about it, he had imagined it, but he hadn't seen it until then.

—I don't like this area, it's full of stray dogs, and they're usually aggressive, it's not the first time I've had to run from them, but the damn superior has sent me to distribute here today, so there it is.

Lucas kept looking around as Romeo dealt with the poor, mostly men, some with beards, and worn out.

—Give me a little more, I'll pay you next time— said one as he tried to grab Romeo's arm.

—Get away, damn it— as he pushed him away. —If you're not careful, they'll take you by the arm. I'm almost done, we've been lucky that there are no dogs around here.

A bearded man can be heard in the background.

—Ray attacks, take everything from him! — as he released a large dog.

The barking could be heard a block away and with it, other dogs came to see what was happening. Lucas and Romeo had to run.

—Damn beasts! I still have 3 grams left.

Romeo knew the area well, fortunately for Lucas, and they hid in a landfill that dumps the waste from the large structure in the center of the city covering a great distance. That dark and metallic structure contained the AI Juan Costana. The area where both ended up was full of recently discarded technological debris; old computers, electronic circuits. Something among all of this caught Lucas's attention.

—What are you looking at among all that garbage? Do you think you're going to find an electric pinocchio and it will activate to start dancing

Romeo and Lucas backed away, what was that? They didn't know, but it was sure to be worse than those dogs. The robotic being spoke, tuning its voice as it spoke.

—I am Vicenta and you have activated me with your voice.

It wore and had the appearance of an old woman, with heels, but its skin was damaged, revealing its metallic structure, a black sphere was visible under its clothing on its chest.

—What voice? — Romeo asked to himself.

—The voice of your young companion, Alvaro. Based on the date on my internal clock, I think I've been asleep for a long time, my skin is repairing, don't worry, I won't always look like this.

The black core caught Lucas's attention, and he stared at it fixedly.

—This is my heart, my core, the source of my operation. My purpose is one and it is to reactivate Juan Costana.

—Stupid robot! Who do you think dictates us? If not that stupid AI. Look at the big screens! — Romeo reprimanded.

—I know what I'm saying! I'm not receiving any strong enough signal from Juan Costana, that image is certainly not him, my sensors are correct, Sofia created me not to fail.

Lucas then reacted, not only did it know his name, but it mentioned a Sofia, the name of his mother.

—What Sofia? How do you know my name? Do you speak of my mother? — Lucas fired.

—Yes Alvaro, I speak of your mother, the one who designed me and gave life to Vicenta.

—Lucas, is Alvaro your real name? How does she know it?

—I don't know.

After a few seconds, Vera and Tomás appeared, who after finishing their part and not seeing either of them, approached the landfill, the main escape place.

—What is that? A walking corpse! — Vera exclaimed.

—I am Vicenta.

—Talk! — Vera exclaimed again.

—I'm not a zombie, I'm an advanced robot.

Vicenta's skin gradually regained its place, although slowly, after the time they spent talking, it was enough to notice.

—What do you want from me? Do you know about my parents?

—You have an important activation key. I haven't known about your parents for a long time unfortunately. But my current function will be to protect you in their absence until the right time comes.

After that, it simply disappeared among the buildings at great speed.

Time passed and Lucas got used to dealing. To do minor jobs and in general to life in the band, he thought a few times about escaping, but he knew it wouldn't help much.

On any good day, Romeo didn't return as usual. The boys, even Lucas, who already saw him as a companion, decided and informed Phoenix.

—Romeo hasn't come back today, it's not normal for him.

Phoenix communicates with some other members and reveals that Romeo has been kidnapped by a drug band in competition with them. That day Romeo went on his own and chose a bad place. Ironically, you could hear in the background "Juan Costana warns you of the spread of street gangs, be careful where you go."

Phoenix creates a small group of three who will be responsible for going after Romeo, they cannot allow rival gangs to do as they please, and take one of their merchants. That was unacceptable! Tomás, who had good hearing and found the perfect place, could hear what Phoenix and the men were talking about. He tells Vera and Lucas about Romeo's location. Lucas says he will help from behind without them seeing him. Tomás says he will accompany him, just like Vera.

At night, the boys follow them from a distance and arrive at one of the small barracks of that band, the Men of God. The three strong men enter the premises and finish the guards as if they were a couple of flies, young lives wasted... In the basement they find Romeo on an old and disgusting mattress. Sedated, thrown and drugged so as not to bother. They take him between two of them. Vera is emotional at that moment to see Romeo, she bumps into the corner where there were a couple of cans. Then a couple of rival criminals appear behind them.

—Who the fuck is there? — Said one of those two who saw them taking a revolver.

The three boys raise their hands. But the criminals who had been watching the location and had been absent for a few minutes know that something is going on there, they look at the premises and do not see any of their companions.

—I see three corpses— says one of them threatening them.

At that moment Vicenta appears from the shadows of the night, ready to reverse the situation and protect

Lucas. They shoot at them and the woman. Vicenta stops the bullets with both hands using armored plates on the palms. Swiftly, she attacks against them and knocks them down with two strong blows to the neck.

Alvaro is afraid at that moment, he does not know if more of the men now lying on the ground, or of Vicenta, that robot with the appearance of an old woman was certainly a prodigious weapon. They watch from a distance until the three allies load into a secluded street in the car they arrived in. Lucas sees that Vicenta has also followed them, he wonders why she is protecting him, what is her purpose?

Again, a man armed who had hidden waiting for his opportunity appears and is about to shoot at Romeo and his rescuers.

—Vicenta, do something, save him! — Lucas shouts.

At that moment Vicenta sees no other option, after the request, she stands in front of the men and stops the bullet that was going directly to one of them.

The men are on alert, they do not understand what has saved them. And they are about to shoot at her, who has apparently appeared out of nowhere.

Lucas, Tomás, and Vera explain the situation to them and make them get into the car.

They arrive at the barracks under the hairdressing salon and tell Phoenix everything that happened, which is angry because they have followed the men and more because they put Romeo in danger.

—I saw how she stopped the bullets, that lady is a machine, part of Juan Costana certainly.

—So you think she's part of Juan Costana and yet you bring her to me?

The men fell silent, they had not realized something so basic. They apologized and said nothing else.

—I'm going to talk to her, alone in private, don't bother.

The men want to tell him it's dangerous, be careful, but they stay silent again.

Vicenta and Phoenix go to the next room. There, they join their foreheads and without measuring words, they communicate. Vicenta's expression is one of happiness. After this, she asks the question that she has told the young people, and she tells everything. The name of Lucas, that she believed that the Juan Costana AI was completely deactivated and that Sofia was her designer.

—They bring Lucas in.

—Alvaro, she will be your protection, beyond that of your small group, she is a true old friend, I will introduce her to the rest of the group later, you have heard deaf to the criticism, in her hands you will be safe. She was secretly created by your mother, with the purpose of deceiving Juan Costana's engineers and ending him.

—But she told me that Juan Costana is deactivated, I don't understand.

—It was just part of the programmed plan, don't pay attention to those words.

That same afternoon, the robot was presented as a support unit, created by the old liberators, Lucas' parents, and its recovery was an important discovery. That they trust it as their leader, even though it is a hated robot, do not compare it to Juan Costana.

—Down with Juancostanism! — They all said in unison.

The days passed and Romeo recovers little by little, he says he already feels well and that he can return to the drug trafficking. The group returns to its task, with Vicenta watching over them. Romeo insists constantly on going alone. They don't understand why, especially considering what happened. Vera watches him instead of fulfilling her task, she is worried. Then she understands, Romeo was drugging, leaving part of his own money and taking the merchandise. Since the day of the kidnapping, he had developed addiction. The distant sound is heard "Julieta drug is highly prohibited, both its distribution and consumption" in the voice of Juan Costana serene and peaceful.

Chapter 1.5: The Great Creation

A dark-skinned woman dressed in a white lab coat observes a perfect black sphere. Next to her, four armed men watch the artifact.

—It's perfect, like a black pearl. — She said to herself, Sophia.

As every week she went down to observe the sphere on the suitcase covered in dark velvet. She did not dare to touch it, she knew well some of its properties and likewise she was unaware of others.

After inspecting it, the box was closed by one of the four men and placed in the armored part of the large computer, there under those metal walls, it remained protected but wasted.

She went up to the laboratory and found her three usual companions, although that day was special. They would take the morning and maybe the whole day thinking about what to do with the sphere.

—We should use it in Sofia's Vicenta project. I have great curiosity about whether it could develop the intelligence of the machine, and then give it to Juan Costana. — Raquel said.

—No! Never that. — Adam said.

Adam's fear was shared by Rafael and Sofía. On the one hand, they feared that Juan Costana had never been conscious and that the core would only function as a battery, and on the other that, if he had it, but that, after receiving the core, he would evolve to such a level that he would become something out of their reach, and leave them behind.

—We must leave it as it is, we play the cards of the fate of Descent, and our own. My great-grandfather would not have accepted it. — Sofía responded firmly.

—We must be grateful that the sphere exists despite not having a body of its own, we must give it one, the Vicenta project is the best option. — Rafael

—We could be giving a body to Dest, with our current technology, it will be perfect. If it is useful to him, he will reward us with something bigger. — Adam explained.

And so Vicenta was born.

—You were right, it is not capable of using the abilities of the nucleus. —Rafael

—That seems to be the case, it is only a high-level AI, it has no consciousness. —Adam

—Consciousness, what is that? — Vicenta said.

—We wouldn't know how to answer that question for you to understand it. — Sofía reflected

—Let's try again, Vicenta, make the chair discontinue its existence.

—How could I do such a thing? — She responded.

—It doesn't matter Vicenta, you will be the great guardian, either way.

And so Vicenta was relegated over the months and subsequent years in Sofia's office. With a smile on her face, but disconnected from reality.

On a fateful day, Rasputin, the resistance hacker against Juan Costana, managed to access the lower nucleus of the computer, responsible for controlling the androids scattered in various tasks around the city. They fell disconnected in mass. The riots of that day went beyond the fall of a system and the emergence of another, it also served for the organized gangs to take control of sectors of the city.

Sofía ran to meet Lucas, Álvaro's father and from whom he receives his pseudonym. But at that moment just a few steps away from the meeting, he was massacred by the bullets of the insurgents, who ended both on the spot. Sofía, in a moment of final clarity, considered what her father or great-grandfather, the creator of Juan Costana, would have done. In that era, he saved the earth, other worlds began to be dictated by Xarus, a systematizer. At first with fear on his part, to end with praise, which led to other worlds, including Earth, to create artificial intelligences imitating him, and with them Descent, which was decided by a figure that exuded peace and serenity, taken from a television program. It was a subject of mockery for some and a great technological miracle for others, but the figure of Juan Costana became that of the great dictator and guardian of Descent over the decades.

Chapter 2: The curtain rises

From the large building that contained the AI, four people spoke looking from a high room with tinted windows. Shepard, Andrés, Hugo and Tristán.

—We should do something special this year. —Shepard

—Certainly, it's about time we show our existence. —Andrés

"It's not Juancostanism, it's new Juancostanism and it hasn't been clear among the population. — Tristán criticized.

—We know it well Tristán. — Shepard replied.

—It will be our 15th anniversary, I think it's a good time. Let's celebrate a parade. We will go ourselves and reveal what the truth is. — Andrés.

—We could end that annoying Anti Juan Costana group with a stroke. —Hugo

On the same day, with the previous days announcing "New Juancostanism, will make a special parade", "Juan Costana wishes you a great day". A great parade with a great imposing golden carriage travels through the center of the city Descent.

The four men greet from the carriage, dressed in face fabrics, and although in appearance it seemed that nothing protected them, an invisible energy field to the eye prevented the entrance of people and protected them from the impact of projectiles. In the applause, Juan Costana is seen greeting with a smile. The large carriage arrives at the main square, a tumult of people cheering the occasion, there are stalls of all kinds in the area, even cotton candy for children and sweets.

The screens go dark and the sound ceases. People notice and silence begins to become authority.

—Citizens, Today I have something very important to tell you. I, Juan Costana, have been deactivated for fifteen years. This is a simple reflection of my being. When the new Juancostanism was announced fifteen years ago, EAUR was born.

The hubbub grew louder. What does our leader Juan Costana say? Is this a tasteless joke? The screens changed and focused on the four men on the carriage.

—They are EAUR, I will stop showing this false figure, I no longer exist, they are the past of the last fifteen years, present and future.

The men of AJC are perplexed, as are the people listening to these words. Some feel deceived, they have faced a ghost for years. Others feel that they have truly won, even though there is nothing new, their only goal was to end the AI, they feel that the ground they walk on and the air they breathe is another at that moment. Phoenix, on the other hand, sees the worst, that the organization is going to crumble, without a clear goal, with a victory turned into old age. Those men with their words had shown a reality that Phoenix did not want to be discovered, not at least at that point. Quickly, he arranged to communicate with as many members as were willing to do so. By group call as in the hairdressing quarters.

—You must know that I, nor any other member knew about this. We must stay united, against the threat, the threat is nothing other than dictators who have mocked us for years. We must achieve justice

The words of Phoenix were lost in the wind with the passing of the days, more and more men and women left the formation, to the point where enemy bands began to take over AJC's sales points without more.

Romeo sees his world and source of income fall, and at that moment only one thing is on his mind: getting more drugs. He only wants Juliet and will do whatever it takes for her. He easily joins the gang that kidnapped him, the Men of God.

Lucas, on the other hand, feels betrayed and feels that Phoenix owes him answers.

—How will I reach my parents! Juan Costana... It may already be only rubble.

—Lucas, it's still too early to lose hope. Your parents could be somewhere. I have to tell you something else. I didn't recruit you just for protection, your voice is an important key, just as it activated Vicenta, it will do the same with Juan Costana. Your parents were not part of any anti-Juan Costana plan. They were a fundamental part of the program.

—I, Vicenta, was certainly created by your mother, but as support for Juan Costana, I don't know the reason why I wasn't activated on time, but my purpose is still the same: to protect you and Juan Costanaism with you. As Phoenix said, your voice is a precious key. We don't know what happened to your parents, but we do know how to find them.

—How?!

—Just as it was planned, but in reverse. We will ask Juan Costana directly when you wake him up. Right now he is in a 1 meter thick metal cylinder, protecting him from any altercations. As far as we know, they haven't been able to break through that barrier in all these years.

Chapter 3: Death and Rebirth

A light but significant request arises for Romeo when he joins the new gang: the location of the AJC's central headquarters.

—What will you give me in return?

—Ten grams of Juliet and admission.

—Enough, you certainly know how to convince young people.

—Only drug-addled young people like you! — the man laughed, irritating Romeo.

Vera, who had been closely following Romeo and worried about her friend, hears him give the location of the place in great detail. She starts to cry, covering her mouth.

—Damn Romeo! For ten grams! Is that what we're worth?!

She quickly runs to warn the headquarters, but a man easily intercepts her. Nothing more was heard of her.

Less than fifteen minutes later, the men arrived. In that place were still Vicenta, Phoenix, and Lucas, along with several other members who tried to defend themselves with no other goal than death. Vicenta goes on alert and manages to deflect the first 3 bullets, but they continue to shoot without caring about anything or anyone. Although Vicenta managed to return some of those bullets, and Phoenix kills a few men with his accurate pistol shot, it was a bloodbath, including Lucas's. One of the bullets had hit him badly. But one was enough.

—Alvaro! No, you won't die here, fortunately, I am still with you.

Lucas was bleeding and didn't stop, he put his hand on the wound, but it wasn't enough. Vicenta hugged him tightly. And Alvaro felt himself slipping away, seeing the light on the ceiling and thinking it was the afterlife.

—Listen carefully, Alvaro, I am going to give you my source of life, the black sphere in my chest. The sphere of continuity, of the Dest system.

At that moment, the nucleus of Vicenta's chest passed like an intangible shadow, from her chest to Lucas's. Vicenta closes her eyes and falls motionless to one side. The seconds pass and the blood stops and the bullet comes out of her body. A strong breath of air brings Lucas back to life. Phoenix explains what happened.

—Now you are not just an ordinary human. You are a mantic of continuity.

—What is that?

—You will understand soon. In any case, only we remain, those who did not flee, have died. I, Phoenix, and you, Lucas, the continuous. You know, I created this organization feeding on hatred of something that was not bad in itself, Juan Costana, is not the horrible despot you have known, they were those four traitors. Your parents and you would have lived happily if it weren't for them. We could leave Descent. Our drug trafficking would not exist, well, it no longer does. There would also be no street gangs, the police would be efficient.

Lucas imagined all that, his parents young and happy, he understood, albeit only halfway, that what he hated was not Juan Costana but everything they did in his name EAUR.

For a few months, when things calmed down, Phoenix and Lucas remained hidden, training the latter in his new power. Which allowed him to return continuously or, conversely, stop the continuity of whatever he wanted. He could stop the bullets that move continuously in the air. Let other people's lives stop continuing, regenerate his body to maintain his continuity. But Phoenix feared that the borrowed power would have limitations when the time came, that a systemizer would come and stop everything, "Or the sphere will reach its limit and crack, and Lucas with it. If they attack the base, it may turn out that the borrowed power is not enough. They need something more or someone else. That's when Phoenix realized.

—Lucas, you must go to Ascent, the city of magic, in Tokyo.

—The city of magic?

—Believe it or not, it's the only magic city you'll ever see in your life. There you must find the black cloak of the immensities. A garment that turns all attacks into nothing.

Lucas was surprised, although once he knew of the power of the core inside him not so much...

—Imagine if we could extend the power of the cloak with the sphere. Return to EAUR in nothing. We don't have another plan, the band will take years, even decades to reform. Although I advise you. Be careful when trying to modify concepts, it could result in a load too high for the sphere, even a systematizer could appear against us.

Lucas accepts and Phoenix helps him escape. Being only one, it was not difficult. Lucas had never been outside the city and that seemed like a kind of paradise to him. He had seen planes in the sky and knew how they looked in photos, but had never been in front of one, much less on board.

Upon arrival he sees posters placed on streetlights and walls everywhere. They were about a tournament, one that was celebrated every few years and had the goal of showing the power of the city, in addition to entertaining its people with shows. The poster had a photo of a man next to a description, Joru, the one who is never defeated. Dressed in a black cloak. Lucas did not think too much about it, could that black cloak be the one he was looking for? He inquired throughout the city and concluded that it was indeed the case. He proceeded to register for the tournament with the money he had left, even the money for the return.

—You also want that coveted prize?

—Prize? What is it?

—Have you fully entered without thinking about it? I suspect you want fame. The staff that stretches indefinitely, that is the prize. If a weakling like you wins,

I would not mind paying you a good amount of money for it.

Lucas did not answer and set out to live quietly in the city until the start of the tournament.

The first fight, the opening one, was as its name indicated only a slightly simple trick to show the strength of the previous champion, Joru's. He would face Iko, the hero of the 6 faces. Invoked only tournament after tournament to let himself be won. Lucas watched this confrontation attentively, he wanted to assure himself of the power of the cloak with his own eyes and see the strengths and weaknesses of Joru.

The referee started the fight and both participants faced each other, each with their respective sword looking at each other. Iko put on a bluish mask, with a scared expression and somewhat childish appearance. And he attacked, he grazed Joru's sword and plunged it into the cloak, which passed the attack as expected into nothing. He drew the sword and parried the attack coming from Joru, with a pose that showed experience. He jumped back and waited for Joru to attack this time. Joru was swift in his thrust and grazed Iko's side, who let himself be wounded on purpose. Iko counterattacked and despite the cloak he wounded Joru in the face, although very lightly, his ability allowed him to leave nothing more than a superficial wound. Joru followed sword blow after sword blow, until he took Iko to the edge of the tatami. Iko was really bored, that fight was not doing him any favor, but he had to fight for his master's summoning rights. He decided at a good moment that it was time to end that.

Joru aimed at his mask, but Iko was the last one who was going to allow that, he deflected the sword with his and positioned his body to be wounded in the shoulder. After that he fell dolorido from the tatami, sobbing with a sad and fake 'Ahhhhh'.

That ridiculous fight pleased the audience, who praised the ability of both, but especially Joru who turned out to be the winner. After a few minutes, Iko got up and changed his mask to a green smiling one that healed his wounds; he stored it again and imitated fatigue towards the barracks.

After an hour, Lucas was called for his fight, against Ander, who used duplicating magic.

The confrontation started. Ander pulled out a knife that he duplicated into three with the help of a magic stone from the many he had in his bag, next to his waist. He stored the one that seemed original and threw them at Lucas, who had gone to participate with only two things, his own power and a sword, firearms were not allowed in duels, it would be too easy, and the opponent would not last long.

Lucas's plan was simple, deflect all enemy attacks with his power and finally bring a hand-to-hand combat until the opponent surrendered or fell from the tatami. He didn't want to kill him, he had never done it and he still had nightmares about the corpses of the revolt in the barbershop. The knives that Ander threw were easily stopped by discontinuing their continuous movement. These fell to the ground no more. As if all of a sudden they had no more energy. Ander was scared and a shiver ran down his body. He didn't know what to think about what had happened, his opponent didn't even touch any of them. He won't send more for the moment, he would attack with the sword, he was right-handed with it, why not end the duel that way? He attacked, but just before he grazed Lucas, the space curved, although it looked like the sword, the sword itself, that curved, something that he could have done as well, if it hadn't occurred to him. If not later, he told himself, if I curve the continuity of the sword I could damage my opponent with the edge of his own sword. That's what he did, while the opponent was still trying to plunge the sword, the edge of this twisted until it hit his hand and opened what would be a scar in the future. He quickly dropped the sword. It ended up twisted on the floor, Ander looked at it fearfully, both for the way it almost cut off part of his hand and for his opponent who didn't seem to be making any gestures to achieve all that. He didn't have another idea, while Lucas was waiting, he threw two of his duplicated knives that this time Lucas deflected from their trajectory and punched Lucas. He hit him full on, Lucas didn't expect to come to blows, but there was only one solution, to do that and finish the fight, he punched Ander back and Ander responded with another, at that moment Lucas slightly modified the continuity of his arm and broke it, He could have made a thousand pieces of his bones, but he was not a barbarian. A little was enough for Ander to scream in pain. This made him desperate and afraid for his life, so he backed away and jumped off the mat, ending the fight in Lucas' favor.

The referee came and raised his hand in victory. The crowd cheered the moment. Lucas had other opponents after a few days of rest, but he withdrew, not showing up, he was more afraid of his own death. Until the fight against Joru, who nobody defeats. Lucas felt unbeatable, untouchable. It was like being in a dream, the power that the Vicenta sphere gave him was perfect, something limitless. But he had never seen its limitations, he was not a systematizer, nor an all-powerful god. Joru and Lucas climbed onto the mat, the presenter and referee began to speak:

—Today we will have the great awaited fight! Beast against beast, steel against steel. Will Lucas be the new champion? Or will Joru continue to be the one who never loses? The final begins!

Both boys faced each other, Lucas, who barely knew about the sword, beyond loose images, had learned more in the previous fight than in his whole life. Joru, on the other hand, was an expert and possessed the black cloak of immensities. Lucas was the first to attack, he plunged his sword into the cloak and confirmed again, but this time for himself that this was the sought-after object, he continued to plunge the sword into the void until he touched the cloak with his hand. At that moment he was ready to win, he only had to extend the nothingness that provided that cloak to

Joru's body, technically he did not kill him, he only "nadified" him, turned him into nothing. Although he did not want to kill him, he knew from the beginning that there was no other option. So that's what he did, he concentrated and wished to turn him into nothing. Only a voice resonated in his head "I Xarus deny it, such power is dangerous" Joru moved away by instinct and Lucas out of fear after hearing that echo in his head and seeing that nothing happened. Was that the voice of a systematizer like Phoenix had warned him? How was he going to win then? He knew that with the sword he had no chance. His mind clouded, and he tried again several times, but each time he touched the cloak and tried it in his mind he heard the same phrase "Denied" with the same voice. Then, looking for another strategy, he realizes. For what? What did it matter to win? He could not use the power of the cloak for his purpose. In addition, he quickly regretted what he tried over and over again, and had overlooked in his mind, "nadifying" him was killing him. He turned halfway to the surprise of Joru who did not understand, and jumped off the mat. Lucas surrendered.

—You win Joru, I have nothing left to do.

—The winner is Joru, the one who never loses! He's done it again! - The referee shouted into the microphone. After this, both young men met behind the scenes. Joru didn't feel like he had had a real victory.

—Here, it's for you, the staff extends indefinitely.

—It's yours, I lost. Why are you giving it to me?

—I don't feel like it was a real victory, plus it's not useful to me. Sell it and you'll get good money out of it. Lucas accepted it, he didn't have any money left to return to Descent, something he hadn't even thought about until then.

—You know, I came for that cloak of yours, if my power had worked as I wanted it to, it would have been mine, but it seems it won't be useful to me.

—I can't give it to you, it's too precious to me.

—It's not necessary, as I said, it wouldn't be useful to me. But I suppose I'll have to find an alternative before I go back.

—I have an idea, take Iko with you. I'll help you steal his summoning knife. I know he's fed up with being used as a puppet, and I've often feared his look, I know he holds more power than the stupid committee lets him use. Joru shows him the safe with a thick glass front that reveals the double-edged golden knife with a diamond gem.

—I'll open it in a moment, I'm good with locks. Just watch out that nobody comes. Lucas obeyed him, he knew that he could probably open it by modifying the concept of closed, but since that fight and after Phoenix's previous words, he began to think that using that power to those limits was too dangerous, or impossible. Joru took about a minute, in which no one came near, he extracted the knife and closed the box, he quickly gave it to Lucas who hid it, he had planned to say that it had been stolen, once Lucas was out of the city, if they suspected him, it would be too late, and Joru didn't want to be involved in it, he would deny everything. Lucas left the city and tested the knife outside of it, in a place he saw abandoned and where no one would bother him.

Iko appeared after following the instructions given by Joru. To make him spin on the ground like a top, and then fly back to his hand.

—Who are you, summoner? Did you steal me? Will I finally get out of that circus?

—I stole you with a little help. I have more interesting purposes for you. Iko knew well that those words meant death and destruction, but he had to do it anyway, he would do it gladly if those he killed deserved it. "Damn the one who separated me from my first master" he thought, he wanted to have had more dignified purposes, he was a hero, a man of fair war.

—My name is Iko - he introduced himself.

—I'm Lucas. After the introductions, he explained everything about Descent. About his parents, about his goal, to end those men, and restore the Juan Costana artificial intelligence, as his parents would have wanted. Iko was glad that his end was to kill dictators, but not so much that he would also impose on another.

Lucas headed to the airport, but forgetting for a moment about the x-ray machines, but after buying the ticket and heading to the machine, he remembers it fortuitously. What to do? It was obvious that they were going to see the knife. So practicing with a lady's suitcase that is about to put a small suitcase in the machine seemed like the best idea to him. He simply made the x-rays pass through the sides of the suitcase and not through it. Discontinuing its trajectory. He succeeded! The small suitcase was not visible on the screen, and apparently the agent at the inspection booth did not notice. But his suitcase was bigger and bulkier, therefore, and unique, in addition. They were not several like hers.

So he take the detour through the center where he placed the knife. Apparently on the screen the suitcase looked nothing suspicious, except for a large rectangular hole in the area. Lucas maintained a serious and tense expression on his face, hoping that the man had not noticed the irregularity. That man, luckily, only looked at the suitcase in general and at the shapes that could be strange, and that square seemed to him that it could be anything but a hole in the vision or in the suitcase. Lucas had succeeded, a small but important achievement. He could have been arrested, had to generate a huge uprising to free himself and it may take a long time to return to Descent, all that went through his head and with reason.

After arriving in Descent he met with Phoenix who was waiting for him at the agreed place. Phoenix did not see him with the cloak as he expected, but he may have carried it in the suitcase.

—Didn't you get the cloak?

—I couldn't use my power with it, I gave up.

—I see, and you haven't brought anyone either, of course who would be enough for such a task. We will have to wait a long time to rebuild the plans.

—Don't get ahead of yourself. If I have brought help. —He said showing the golden summoning knife.

—A golden summoning knife! You don't know how few there are, their help could be greater than that of a small army.

—Well, well, let's not exaggerate, but yes, with it we can reach the central computer.

—Show me the hero.

Lucas placed the tip of the knife on the ground and rotated it. This same effect was picked up and after a few moments Iko appeared in that same place.

—Hello again and I see that there is company. A cyborg, I hadn't seen one in a long time.

—What cyborg? There are only the three of us here.

—Doesn't it serve you with my look towards him? Did he deceive you, new master? I can see the metal part that covers his circuits, even a small fragment of electronics.

Lucas didn't understand why Iko was saying that. Why would he lie?

—You see my eyes, they are green, in your world it may be something normal, but in my world that means that you see beyond the normal. — He says pointing at both of them.

—Phoenix, say something.

—I think the time has come for you to know a little more about me. I am a part connected wirelessly to Juan Costana. I am Juan Costana, but only as I said a small fragment of his Ego. I have kept myself functioning all these years at a ridiculous capacity, I had to hack my own being at the moment I was disconnected, but I am not able to initiate myself completely. I have not lied to you, I don't know your parents. I cannot access that part of my memory, and I cannot reactivate myself with your voice from here. This is the body of a man who serves me as a puppet.

—You have something hidden from me master, my eyes do not fail.

Lucas didn't know what to say at that moment, he felt deceived despite there being no really important information in relation to what he wanted, his parents.

—Do you have any memories of my parents?

—I have some of your father fixing circuits in his room, seen through my cameras. These are memories that I can still access, but the key information is sealed, under complex systems.

Lucas decides that he needs to meditate and rest, he asks Iko to leave and with the knife in his hands he is ready to disappear until the next day. He felt that he should have insisted more, but in Phoenix's tone and in his figure he did not see any falsehood, so the best thing was to let it be.

Chapter 4: There was a reform

The next day Lucas appears before Phoenix, annoyed, but still with the feeling that he must end all of this.

—Iko do you have any ability to dodge or stop bullets.

—I can attract them towards my sword with the mask of the exuberant.

—And can you return them?

—Yes, but not in these conditions. I can use the mask of revenge to return received attacks, but I cannot attract them to my sword at the same time.

—I really should have gotten that cloak.

—We don't really need it. Lucas focus on deflecting the bullets towards Iko's sword, and Iko use the mask of revenge to return them. It will only be a moment until we finish off the guards.

—I see it as feasible. — Iko responds.

—Lucas, do you know which song is true?

—About that piano, right?

—Yes, that one.

Phoenix stayed behind watching that no one came to interrupt. Both boys acted according to the plan, they called the attention of the guards who were appearing and quickly finished them off. Iko did not mind at all having to kill, but Lucas was feeling more and more guilty despite them being his enemies. After entering they go up to the seventh floor and there a huge armored door opens thanks to the remaining power of Juan Costana.

For a moment Lucas, upon seeing it, thought that they had lost, but the door only took a few seconds to open enough for both of them to sneak inside. It was a large room full of computer terminals, completely isolated within the building, impeccable for 15 years. Near the middle was a huge cylinder, hiding the main part of the computer Juan Costana. There, Lucas recited the song.

"Behind the white keys, the power of the mind

Transcended borders, eternal borders

Written in full scores

Under the eternal light, man was God and God was man..."

After those words, all those teams turned on, and with them a large screen more typical of a movie at the back of the room. Showing all together with those of the streets, the face once again of Juan Costana. It could be heard even in the echo:

—Juan Costana back, governor of our city

At that moment the ninth floor room where the four governors were, closed. They who saw the image of Juan Costana from the large window, immediately understood what had happened. Their greatest fear was present at that moment. Anguish flooded their faces. "What do we do?" "Calm down, I'm calling! They will come for us and this will only be a bad time"

From the huge screen the face of Juan Costana looked attentively at Lucas, and spoke:

—You are free to ask.

—My parents, where are they? What happened to them?

—Now that my memory is complete I know, but are you sure you want the answer?

A shiver ran down Lucas's body and with a stuttering voice, imagining the answer he said:

—Yes, tell me.

—Your parents died fifteen years ago during the arrival of the new Juanism, the four men who have proclaimed themselves as EAUR are responsible.

Lucas screamed as loudly as his lungs could, even Iko next to him was scared of such a reaction.

—Take me to them, Iko you can go.

—Iko returned to the golden knife and Lucas left the room, which closed again behind him. There in the hallway an elevator was waiting for him. He entered it and arrived at the ninth floor.

Together in front, when he left it, a single door. It was closed with armored metal. Lucas approached and this protection folded in, behind it a normal door, it opened easily with a twist of the wrist.

—Help, help is coming! — Exclaimed one of the four.

Lucas showed his teeth, in an expression of unstoppable fury, his eyes, on the other hand, although determined, were overflowing with tears that ran down his face. Although his face could barely be seen, as he looked at the floor.

—Who are you?

—Get out of there!

Lucas looked at them fixedly with that face and closed the door behind him.

The more they tried to defend themselves the worse it was for them, Lucas had no hesitation, nor did he feel any guilt at that moment. After silence fell, Lucas opened the door again, full of red. He sat on the ground and rested.

Juan Costana, in all of this, had sent the machines of the underground complex, police, soldiers, administrative workers, even all the machines commanded by him, to recover the city from gangs, mafias, and all sympathizers of EAUR that they knew of, at gunpoint, and despite the constant shooting of one and the other. In the background, there was an echo that penetrated the soul.

"Juan Costana, governor of our city."

www.ingramcontent.com/pod-product-compliance
Lightning Source LLC
La Vergne TN
LVHW010509160826
845677LV00012B/2760

* 9 7 9 8 3 6 9 8 8 8 0 1 8 *